I0520308

HOUSE OF HARWOOD

A Novella

Olivia Batker Pritzker

Serealities Press
www.serealities.com

Copyright © 2014 Olivia Batker Pritzker
All rights reserved.

ISBN: 0692268154
ISBN 13: 9780692268155
Library of Congress Control Number: 2014914333
Serealities Press, Birmingham, AL

1

The cold marble statue in the entrance hall of the Harwood mansion had looked down without pity on the members of the family for as long as the grand house had stood: an angel, perfectly carved, with laughing eyes and a cold mouth. It had seen it all—illicit rendezvous, shouting matches in the entryway, whispered conversations, people sneaking past at night and again the next morning. The angel had witnessed breakdowns, backhanded deals, and blowouts, and had stood rigid and unmoving through it all, just as the Harwood name had endured its sometimes torrid, often public, and always layered history. The angel—frigid, imposing, perfect—was their protector, and the standard to which all members of the Harwood family held themselves. Not one of them had not at some point walked past the carved beauty and lamented his or her own imperfections, or else secretly reveled in them, defying their stone guardian. The angel was as impossible to live up to as the Harwood name itself, but the family members had continued to try, at least in appearance, for generations.

❈ ❈ ❈

John James Harwood lowered his eyes humbly to the extravagantly carved mahogany dining table, his gaze lingering on the rows of polished, monogrammed silver, gilded bone china, and crystal goblets. Then he cleared his throat. "We thank you, Lord, for the food you have put in front of us today, and for allowing us to be together. Amen."

"Amen," echoed the rest of the family, heads bowed.

The knives were sharpened, the chandelier sparkled, and the members of the Harwood clan were dressed in their finest silks and wools, a bounty of warm autumn tones to celebrate the harvest season and the fact that this Thanksgiving, the family business was as rich and prosperous as anyone could remember.

"In keeping with the Harwood family tradition, it's time for each of us to name something we're thankful for," said John James. "And *then* we can tuck into Sophia's delicious meal." He winked roguishly at the dark-haired woman sitting beside him. She looked so dry and pale that she seemed to have poured every last drop of her life into the succulent feast before them. "*Also* in keeping with our tradition, as the head of this family, I will begin." John James shifted his stately gaze to each member of the family in turn. "I am thankful for all of you sitting here in front of me. I couldn't ask for anything more."

Two sets of eyes locked across the table. A mouth twisted into a slight smirk.

Sophia spoke next. Eyes downcast, she murmured her agreement with her husband; she, too, gave thanks for the joys and comforts of being surrounded by family. There were no smirks following her soft words, but did a foot ever so lightly tap another?

After Sophia was Victoria, John James's sister. Her plump, plum-painted lips proudly declared her threefold thanks: for her charming husband, for her enduring good looks, and for her new Mercedes. She then looked eagerly around the room, hungry eyes searching for proof of jealousy on the faces of her family members.

With one hand placed proprietarily on the back of her neck, her husband, Victor, made a joke about also being thankful for his wife's enduring good looks. He then looked over at his niece, Tanya. "I am also thankful for life's little surprises."

Tanya looked down at the table. "Pass," she murmured. No one was surprised.

Victoria took a gulp of wine.

It was Amy's turn. John James's younger daughter often made it clear that she was not thankful at all—that she appreciated nothing, took nothing for granted, and trusted no one—yet at the moment her baby face and honey eyes were the picture of innocence. Even her long straight hair hadn't allowed a single strand out of line. She beamed sweetly around the table. "I'm thankful for all the good-hearted people who care about me. I wouldn't know what to do without my family." John James gave a terse smile that did not reach his eyes.

Before having the last word, as was her due, Clarissa Harwood looked slowly around the table, her gaze pausing on each family member in turn. The perfect vision of a sweet old lady, Granny was nevertheless sharp and ruthless, and she fiercely protected her own. "I'm thankful for this family, which I have built, and for the continuing strength to protect it. May you all get exactly what you deserve."

❀ ❀ ❀

The Harwood family was an institution, one of the few old families to have been living in the town of Coventry since its founding centuries ago. The Harwoods had built their fortune in the glass eye industry; Clarissa's grandfather, an irascible glassblower named Augustus Harwood, had developed a process for custom tinting the orbs for a perfect match. Since the boom years of the two world wars, Harwood Industries had held the nationwide monopoly on ocular prosthetics, and the Harwood glass eye factory was the single-largest employer in Coventry.

As soon as the money had started rolling in, Gus had donated heavily to the city, and as a result the Harwood name was engraved on the library, hospital, schools, and various parks and squares. Everyone in town knew the names of the Harwood family members past and present, eagerly repeating the salacious and sobering details of their lives and the scandals that plagued them. Only a few people were old enough to remember when Anita Harwood had run away with the milkman, but most of the town's older generation still remembered hearing tales about old Gus Harwood with a shudder, and almost everyone had heard stories of how he treated Emily and why she had been sent away.

There hadn't been a major scandal in decades; to outsiders, it might have appeared that the Harwoods had enjoyed peaceful, respectable, and unremarkable lives for the past few generations. Not that there hadn't been plenty of minor transgressions and extravagant spectacles for the public to gossip about. For example, when Victoria had married Victor, articles and photos covering their lavish wedding set young girls and women swooning over the excesses of flowers and finery. Victoria looked like a princess, everyone whispered, and Victor was her delightful prince. It was a grand affair, and people spoke of it even years later in tones of awe.

And yet, as Victoria herself had bitterly pointed out several years later, their wedding had seemed a pedestrian affair compared with that of her brother, John James, to the lovely Catherine Fields. Their engagement party alone had been a thing of gossip and wonder. Had there really been live peacocks strutting about the grounds? Did champagne really flow from the mouth of a cherub statue carved from the finest crystal? And—most remarkably—had John Sr. really shed a tear during his toast upon seeing his son so happily betrothed to the woman of his dreams?

By their wedding day, Catherine had become something of a local celebrity. It would be only a small overstatement to say that everyone in the town had been waiting to see whom the handsome

Harwood heir would marry. In choosing Catherine, it seemed that he had filled all their expectations and more.

The wedding celebration had lasted for an entire weekend, during which time the town had been almost completely immobilized by the festivities. Stores closed early. Streets were blocked off. Harwood Industries gave everyone that Saturday off—with pay. The better part of the police force was appropriated to control the crowds, and to make sure that no uninvited guests crashed the event, although both the chief of police and the mayor were on the guest list. The procession from the church to Harwood House had all the gaiety and spectacle of a parade. Music filled the air, spilling over the walls from the gardens and lawns and wafting into the neighboring streets. In a show of conspicuous generosity, the Harwoods had ordered a second wedding cake made for the commoners, wheeling the five-hundred-pound, seven-tiered confection outside the ivy-covered walls that embraced the mansion. The tiny bride and groom gazing down from the top tier stood higher than the wrought iron gates, and Gilbert the kitchen aid had been given the task of climbing a ladder in his coat and tails to cut the massive cake and distribute it in equal portions to whomever wanted a slice.

John James's second wedding, the one to Sophia, had been considerably more understated. The ceremony had been modest and—dare it be said?—rather ordinary. The townspeople hadn't really known how to react to the occasion, and offers of toasts, gifts, and congratulations were tinged with a somber awkwardness that was palpable. The bride's and groom's demeanors hadn't helped to ease the tension. Sophia had been quietly appreciative, murmuring her thanks to anyone who offered felicitations, her manner more like that of someone just awakened from a deep sleep than like that of a bubbly new bride. John James had been noticeably reserved, accepting congratulations and thanking people in a flat, almost mechanical tone; he was hardly recognizable as the same man who'd laughed and danced at his first wedding.

At that reception, Clarissa noticed that while the ill-prepared Sophia dutifully struggled to hold court, John James slipped away from the crowds for nearly an hour. She'd found him sitting in a quiet room playing with his toddler daughter, Tanya, who was giggling obliviously in her pale yellow dress. With a strong but sympathetic word or two, Granny Clarissa had coaxed her son back to the party. At John James's second wedding, only Victor had seemed in excellent spirits, dancing and drinking and shouting joyously of his love for the happy new couple. The celebration had ended early. When John James and Sophia had returned to Harwood House together after their brief honeymoon, the mansion somehow seemed even emptier than before.

Years had passed since that uneasy occasion, however. Now John James's two daughters were both nearly of an age when the townspeople could fully expect another grandiose Harwood celebration, another new family member to gossip about, and—they could always hope!—another scandal.

❀ ❀ ❀

Tanya poked at the mound of toasted stuffing sitting on her plate, contemplating the various chopped vegetables mixed in. Celery, onion, mushrooms…was that parsley? She could feel her Aunt Victoria's eyes boring into her, and she determinedly kept her gaze locked downward. Couldn't Victoria at least *pretend* not to hate her when everyone else was around? Not that her antipathy was such a secret.

"Ready to have your eyes clawed out with fake nails?" Amy had asked earlier that day, her eyes lighting up as she imagined the scenario; Amy always took great pleasure in watching her older sister suffer. Tanya began sorting her food into little piles on her plate—bits of mushroom, bits of celery…

Of course, as Tanya was constantly reminded, she and Amy were only half siblings. As much as her Aunt Victoria hated her, Tanya was sure that her stepmother Sophia hated her even more. Tanya always tried to empathize with people, to see things from the others' points of view, so she supposed that if she were in Sophia's shoes she might dislike having to raise someone else's daughter, too. After all, wasn't Tanya just a reminder to Sophia that she was not John James's first wife? But as much as Tanya tried to understand Sophia's distance, she had always felt more than a little like Cinderella.

The first time she had read the story of Cinderella, she had immediately identified with the protagonist. Everything fit: the pitiless stepmother, the sister who tormented her, the kind but absent father. As she got older, she kept returning to the story, laughing at the thought of staid, imperious Clarissa as the smiling, singing fairy godmother. Tanya's childhood interactions with Granny were primarily lessons about the proper way to do this or that—pour tea, compose a letter, sit with perfect posture in ladylike fashion. Afternoons with Granny had always been boring at best and mildly terrifying at worst; Tanya remembered one excruciatingly hot afternoon spent on the terrace with Amy while Granny drilled them both on the names and positions of their ancestors. Tanya still couldn't understand what good a thorough knowledge of the Harwood family tree would do her, but she concentrated and memorized dutifully nonetheless. Meanwhile, Amy had sat off to the side in the shade, brushing her long hair, sipping lemonade, and confusing Edward Harwood II and his nephew Bartholomew with bored indifference.

Tanya's favorite childhood memories all seemed to feature her father. On her seventh birthday, for example—one of several that Sophia had conveniently "forgotten" about—John James had come into the sunroom where Tanya was playing with her dolls, alone. With a twinkle in his eye, he had presented her with a present so large he had to wheel it in. Tanya remembered everything about that moment—how beautiful the shiny pink wrapping paper had been, drawn up with the green satin bow…how happy she'd been that her father had remembered her birthday…the anticipation she'd felt as she tore off the wrapping paper…and, of course, the joy that had elicited a squeal of delight when she'd unwrapped the life-sized stuffed pony on wheels. But she would also never forget seeing Sophia's sad face framed in the doorway, her stepmother holding two-year-old Amy in her arms—both mother and daughter utterly ignored by her husband. That night, she'd heard Sophia crying in her father's bedroom. The next day, Sophia "forgot" about both Tanya's breakfast and her lunch.

It was always Amy, never Tanya, who was invited by their aunt, Victoria, on various outings—to the candy store when they were young, or to the salon as they left their childhoods behind. Aunt Victoria seemed to enjoy paralyzing her older niece with a hostile glare as she watched Amy excitedly get her coat, as if daring Tanya to ask to join them. Although Tanya could almost understand Sophia's hatred, she still didn't know why Victoria disliked her so much.

❖ ❖ ❖

On Tanya's left, Amy was spooning gravy onto her mashed potatoes and telling Granny something in a low tone with her usual sweet smile and calculating eyes. Granny, nodding approvingly, poured herself more wine.

To Tanya's right, John James attacked his turkey with silent, ruthless energy. He looked up when Victor addressed him, eyes hard as he continued to slice his meat.

"How's the market treating you, John?"

Victoria shifted her gaze to her husband, sweetly serving him a portion of yams while Granny refilled his wineglass and John James speared a piece of turkey onto Victor's plate.

"I'm doing all right, Victor. I can't complain."

Victor laughed heartily and took a long gulp of wine. "You're always doin' all right, Johnny. Wish you could pass a little of that luck on to me."

John James smiled coldly. "You never know what the future will bring, of course, but success is not about luck. You have to take control of your life, Victor. Eliminate uncertainty, and you won't need luck." He turned toward his wife and offered her the plate of turkey. Although she shook her head, he forked a few pieces of white meat onto her plate anyway, and then took more for himself.

Victoria ran her red nails through her expensively styled hair. "Now, John. Not *everyone* likes to be controlled." She glanced meaningfully at Sophia, who was quietly and dutifully eating her turkey.

John James sneered contemptuously at his sister. "You don't seem to mind being taken care of."

Victoria flushed and opened her mouth to retort, but decided against it and took another gulp of wine. As feisty as Victoria was, she'd never been able to stand up to her brother. She'd never been able to stand up to any man. Some people, somewhat cruelly, speculated that that was why she'd married Victor Alden.

Victoria had always loved chasing boys, and even more so being chased by them. She'd giggle and toss her bouncy, highlighted hair, and they would flock to her, bestowing compliments and gifts and showering her with attention. But beneath her sunny, flirtatious exterior, Victoria had always suffered a running undercurrent of doubt, a deep insecurity that stemmed from the persistent feeling that she was pursued for her money and looks, not for who she really was.

As she got older, the pressure to settle on someone had been strong. Granny was no fool; she knew that the sooner Victoria married, the sooner certain kinds of scandal could be successfully averted. Around Victoria's eighteenth birthday, she had met Victor. He was different from the overly polished, casually rich, good-mannered boys she usually batted her false eyelashes at. He made her feel as though he was interested in *her*—not her looks or money—and he was exciting, in a new and very different way. Victor was much more demonstrative about how he felt about her, too, holding her hand and kissing her in public. Once he had even ridden his motorcycle to her house in the middle of the night and tossed pebbles at her window until she slipped out to meet him in the garden. He kept her on her toes; she had to work for his affection, which she wasn't used to doing. Maybe that was why he gave her such a thrill.

Victor wasn't from what the Harwoods considered to be a "good family," and when Victoria first introduced him, Granny and John Sr. had expressed their doubts. But they soon conceded that the young man was intelligent, would make handsome sons, and cleaned up nicely, wearing the right clothes, adopting the right hairstyle, and using the right fork. He knew enough to air-kiss Granny on the cheek and compliment her prized rose garden, and to talk finance and Scotch and other important things with John Sr. He was respectful, eager to learn about the family business, and seemed willing to work hard, too—a quality lacking in many of the rich, privileged boys who aspired to become Victoria's husband. When Victor had finally gone to Harwood House to ask Victoria's father for her hand in marriage, permission had been granted.

"Victoria, John—behave," said Granny dryly. She squeezed Amy's arm. "I won't have that kind of bickering at this table. Surely there are other topics of conversation. Amy was just telling me abou—"

A clatter of silverware interrupted her sentence. The family collectively turned to look toward Victor. Even redder in the face than usual, he was pawing the tablecloth, trying to retrieve the knife he had dropped. He gave up and seized his water glass instead, spilling some in the rush to drink. With his other hand, he unbuttoned his top collar button and loosened his tie slightly, grinning weakly. "S-s-sorry, all. Guess I've had too much wine, although I didn't think I...Victoria? I feel kinda dizzy..."

Victoria pursed her lips and refilled Victor's water glass.

John James narrowed his eyes and looked away, focusing on buttering a roll.

Granny smiled and gave a forgiving wave of her hand. "Don't worry, Victor. It's a holiday, after all. Have as much as you like. Would you like some more potatoes?"

Victor didn't answer. His pink face had turned a dark purplish color. Clutching his throat, he shoved his chair back and moved to get up from the table, took a jerky step to the side, and collapsed to the floor.

"Victor!" Victoria screamed and leapt out of her chair.

John James stood up and moved toward his brother-in-law's inert form. He searched for a pulse. After trying the man's neck and both wrists, he looked up with a bland expression. "I believe he's dead."

There was a long, horrified pause. Then the silence was broken by Victoria's wail as she threw herself over her husband's body. Then she whirled to point an accusing finger. "You!" she shrieked, wild-eyed. "You did this. I know you did!"

2

From the start, there were rumors about Victor's infidelity, but nothing solid enough to qualify as an actual scandal. There had been some incident with a hotel maid in Barcelona, but that wasn't local, and facts were blurry. There had been talk about Angela, the personal assistant Victoria had hired and almost instantly fired with the vague explanation that Angela was "untrustworthy." Then there was old Admiral Parker's wife Doreen, whose eye contact with Victor at the City Transportation benefit luncheon had been a little too intense, but nothing had been proven there, either. Either Victor was better at covering his indiscretions than he looked, as John James suspected, or he really was guilty of nothing, as Victoria always maintained.

Whatever the reason, though, over the years Victoria had become less trusting and forbearing, and far more possessive and jealous. Her materialism, which had once seemed like nothing more than a method of assessing boys' relative interest in her, now seemed like a lifeline she clung to, as if she believed that youthful happiness could be assured with just one more lavish present from Victor. Her appearance became less and less real, with her new mask mirroring the denial and skewed outlook she had on life. Her long, glossy, chemically treated hair, her shiny fake nails, and her plastic-smooth face gave her the unnatural appearance of a life-size Barbie™ doll, flawlessly color-coordinated and relentlessly accessorized to create a glossy, perfect life.

Some people wondered how she really felt under those layers of makeup and expensive clothes. Was she content with her marriage, with her life? Had she resigned herself to turning the occasional blind eye, burying her feelings of jealousy and betrayal under caked-on foundation, blush, and mascara, or drowning them in hundred-dollar bottles of wine? Or was she looking for a way to escape?

※ ※ ※

John James raised his eyebrows a fraction of an inch and stepped away from the body. "Really, Victoria? We all know how melodramatic you can be, but accusing me of murdering your husband?" With a look of disgust, he returned to his seat at the head of the table and took a long drink of water. He pressed his napkin to his lips, surveying his shocked family over the edge of the fine linen. "He took too big a bite, I'm sure, knowing his uncouth manners, and choked to death." When no one spoke, he sighed and continued. "Still, I suppose we need to call an ambulance. If nothing else, they can at least get him out of here."

This elicited another wail from Victoria, who had been desperately slapping her dead husband's cheek in a futile effort to wake him. Her shining, mascara-smudged eyes gazed up feverishly at her brother. "John," she gasped. "How could you?"

John James pushed his chair back and stood up once more, tossing his napkin down on the table. He turned to walk out of the room, but was stopped by Victoria's shriek. "Don't walk away from me! I've been waiting for something like this for years! I know all about him and *her!*" She whirled around to face Tanya. Tanya jumped in her seat, a look of horror on her face. Victoria shouted at her. "You! Did you know? About your mother?"

"That's enough." John James's voice could have frozen hell. "Victoria, don't you dare speak about my wife. Ever." Sophia flinched. John James turned to Tanya, who was trembling from head to toe. "Tanya, your mother was a wonderful woman and I loved her very much. When I lost Catherine, I thought it was the end of my life…" His voice wavered. Then he seemed to recover himself, and his voice found its iron stateliness once again. "Until I met my salvation." He nodded toward Sophia, smiling briefly. "Life goes on, Victoria. There's no need to cast blame, reopen old wounds, or dig into things that have long been buried."

He left the room to place two calls. The first was the obligatory but pointless call to the ambulance service. The second was to the family lawyer. The response to both calls was immediate. The EMTs arrived quickly and Victor's body was, indeed, taken away. And the family lawyer appeared in person to announce that he would take care of everything. John James clapped him on the back and shook his hand, then offered him a brandy. When the lawyer assured the grieving widow that he would personally handle everything with the police and the press, she broke down anew.

"The police?" Victoria wailed. "And the press…reporters… oh, oh dear, will I be on camera?"

The turkey and trimmings grew cold on the table as the Harwoods, by unspoken mutual agreement, all drifted into separate rooms.

❖ ❖ ❖

The coroner, disturbed from his own Thanksgiving feast by a call from the Harwood family lawyer, agreed to conduct a post mortem immediately, as a personal favor to the mayor, who was a golfing partner and close friend of John James. The pathologist drove to the examination fully expecting to find nothing more exciting than a rogue turkey bone lodged in the man's throat or, at best, signs of a heart attack. The coroner's dark mood at being pulled away from a delicious apple pie and a moderately diverting football game was not helped by his conviction that this would be just another premature but otherwise natural death. So he was secretly delighted to find that not only was the cause of death in this case not routine, but it was also downright exotic. Victor Alden had been poisoned. Eventually the results would confirm that in addition to the expected stomach contents—cranberry sauce, green bean casserole, potatoes and gravy, the usual fare—was a lethal dose of a rare South American poison.

❈ ❈ ❈

John James, unlike Victoria, had been quiet and serious in his youth, and quickly learned to cover his shyness around girls with a superior aloofness. He and his sister were never close; he treated her as an inferior and constantly lorded his seriousness over what he called her "female frivolity."

"Going out again tonight, Vicky?" he would ask with dry contempt. "Who's the lucky boy this time?"

When Victoria would chatter excitedly to Granny about this or that new suitor, John James would scowl and look away, or make some withering comment sure to send Victoria into a gale of tears. John James was good looking and well mannered, and local society girls were forever winking and blinking at him, dropping so many things for him to chivalrously return that he began experiencing back pain. But he always rebuffed their eager advances, crushing their hopes with a cold word or two. He had once reduced poor Maisie Ashbury to tears by rejecting her invitation to see a double feature at the local cinema, saying that even sitting through just one movie with her would be a waste of his time.

When Granny gently inquired as to whether he could do her a favor and escort Sybil Townsend's granddaughter to a charity picnic, he gave a long-suffering sigh and replied that he had far more important things to do than frolic in the sun with some silly girl, but as usual he did what he was repeatedly told was his duty. The society circuit ceased feeling like the eighth circle of hell that day—the day he met Catherine Fields.

It had been a breezy summer day and the family was sponsoring yet another picnic benefit for yet another new hospital wing dedicated to yet another grim-faced, long-dead Harwood. Granny was in her element, and even John Sr. had stopped by to say a few words before retreating to his offices. The teenaged John James was playing the role he had been raised to play, mingling with the other high-society offspring, smiling at and chatting with the daughters, talking earnestly with the sons. It bored him to death, and he wished he could be anyone else—the head surgeon of the hospital, the mayor of the town—attending to important matters instead of wasting his time with this superficial nonsense. He couldn't stand the way it made him look, having to sit there laughing at some stupid joke, trying to project an air of comfort by rolling up his sleeves and loosening his tie. John Sr. wouldn't have been caught dead sitting on the ground, even on a picnic blanket, eating a slice of pie.

John James had endured just about all he could stand of praising finger sandwiches and talking golf handicaps when he'd spotted a girl he'd never seen before. It was a cliché to end all clichés—the glinting sunlight on her hair, the light illuminating her face as she turned, laughing, toward him. The moment seemed to happen in slow motion, and even the colors around her seemed unreal, like a hand-tinted photograph. How could her eyes be that green, her dress that white, her hair that chestnut brown? When she smiled at him, for the first time in his life John was glad to be exactly who he was: the young, good-looking heir to the substantial Harwood fortune.

Catherine came from a well-to-do family from a neighboring town. She'd been raised to be a perfect society wife, and she had the charm, grace, and intelligence to succeed. She and Granny instantly hit it off, while Victoria instantly disliked her, hating how everyone fawned over her—and how much Granny and John Sr. admired her.

At John James's side, Catherine had delivered on the promises her upbringing and perfect bearing suggested—she'd given birth to a beautiful daughter they named Tanya, who inherited her mother's sweet nature. Catherine proved to be the perfect Harwood wife, hosting dinners and parties and graciously attending to the family's place in society. As for John James, something had clearly changed in him. He worked hard to take his place as the next in line, the new head of the family, sustaining the fortune and the family's role as an institution in the town. In the office, he had the same hard-as-nails manner as ever. Everywhere else, though, it was clear to everyone that he was deeply, hopelessly in love.

Alone in his study, John James poured himself a Scotch and picked up a photo of Catherine from his desk. It showed a petite woman, radiant in heels and a short, summery dress backlit by the sun, gazing lovingly down at the smiling dark-haired infant in her arms. Catherine had short-cropped chestnut hair, jade-green eyes, and an easy, aristocratic smile. To the outside world, she was the perfect wife, hostess, and mother, down to the perfect flourished script of her handwritten thank-you notes. Even her suicide had been perfect. John James sighed and downed his Scotch in one gulp, remembering that awful day.

He'd been working late at the Harwood offices when he'd received the call from his mother. He'd been so immersed in the figures he was going over—there'd been strong interest in their new line of LED pupil dilators that quarter—that he hadn't picked up on the strange hesitancy in her voice or the fact that she normally would have been in bed by that hour. So when his mother had told him that Catherine's BMW had been found, twisted and smoldering, at the bottom of the nearby gorge, it had taken a moment or two for the stabbing pain in his stomach and the shortness of breath to begin.

"John?" Granny's voice had floated over the phone. "Are you there?"

John James was unable to answer. After a few moments, Granny continued softly.

"John, I'm so sorry. They haven't found a...body." Granny hesitated. "The police aren't saying for sure what happened, but they think that—well, judging by the state of the car and the rapids in the gorge—they think it must have been either incinerated or swept away down the river. Of course, they have people searching, but I wouldn't trust to hope. She couldn't have survived." Though his only response had been shallow breathing, Granny pressed on. "Anyway, come home, John. We're all here. Just come home." She gently clicked the receiver into place and sighed.

There was a dull ringing in John James's ears. Catherine, dead? How was it possible? He had seen her alive and well just that morning, still half asleep as he left for work, looking calm and beautiful, wearing nothing but her lavender nightgown—her jewelry lay on the nightstand, casually removed after the family dinner they'd had for Tanya's birthday the night before. He couldn't understand it. Catherine had driven around that bend above the gorge hundreds of times. It wasn't even a particularly sharp turn, and it hadn't been raining or foggy. In fact, it had been one of the clearest nights in a long time.

After the phone call, John had sat immobile in his office for what seemed like hours. He didn't remember how he had gotten home, barely remembered the murmured shock and condolences of his family members, and even less of his conversation with the police chief, who told him in a hesitant, deeply apologetic tone that all the signs pointed toward suicide.

John James downed his Scotch and poured a third. He remembered the day as if it had been yesterday—the moment of realization, the horror, the grief. Tanya crying, Granny comforting them both with soothing words about time and healing and everything happening for a reason. Well, he didn't understand the reason, and time had not healed his pain. It still hurt, all these years later. As John James finished his Scotch and refilled the glass a fourth time, his thoughts turned to Victoria's ridiculous accusation. His sadness turned to anger as he recalled his sister's high-pitched voice demanding of Tanya, "Did you know about your mother?"

John James banged his fist down on his broad mahogany desk. Shortly before Tanya was born, Victoria had approached him directly with that same sordid accusation, and he'd flatly refused to listen. Everyone knew that Victor cheated on Victoria with everyone from naïve hotel maids to bored society wives; Victor got around faster than the gossip that trailed behind him. John James felt sorry for his sister—although it was her own damned fault, since she had married that boor in the first place—but whatever anger or bitterness she felt about her own marriage, he refused to allow it to affect his. Victoria had no right to cast aspersions on his wife just because her husband was a louse. It didn't help anyone for her to blame other people for the things that were wrong in her own life.

And now, the same allegation had surfaced again, along with an even more ludicrous accusation—that he had murdered Victor. How dare Victoria accuse him of knocking off her stupid, worthless husband? As if he could be bothered.

❈ ❈ ❈

Tanya washed and Amy dried, and at first the two girls didn't speak. Amy wanted to discuss the events of the afternoon—certainly they were the most exciting they'd witnessed firsthand! But Tanya seemed strangely subdued, even in shock. When Amy had innocently inquired what was wrong, Tanya had snapped at her—a rare occurrence.

"God, Amy!" Tanya turned around so suddenly that Amy was sprayed with flecks of foamy, lavender-scented soap. "Uncle Victor just dropped dead in front of our eyes. Dad said he was poisoned! Don't you understand what that means? Not only did our uncle just die, but someone in our family probably killed him! Doesn't that concern you? And just after…I mean, just before…" Tanya's eyes filled with tears and she seemed overwhelmed for a moment. "I mean, God…poor Victor!" She turned back to silently scrubbing the roasting pan with vigor.

Amy studied her half sister intently. Tanya had always been the softhearted, sympathetic one, so it didn't surprise Amy that she was getting herself all worked up. Personally, Amy didn't see anything heartbreaking about Victor's death. No one had liked him that much anyway. Her father always looked at him with barely concealed hatred, Granny interacted with him as little as possible, and Amy suspected that even Victoria, for all her wailing and moaning, hadn't really liked her husband.

Amy had never cared much for Victor, either. She found him kind of creepy, and preferred to visit her aunt's three-story cottage only when Victor was away. Then, she and Aunt Victoria would gossip about the other family members while her aunt gave her makeup tips and they drank virgin strawberry daiquiris together. Mourning Victor's death seemed colossally boring to her.

The idea that someone in their family might be a murderer, however, was a much more interesting prospect. Amy would much rather discuss that possibility than waste time pretending to be sad about Victor. But Tanya's apparent shock and grief was tiresomely unshakeable, so Amy resigned herself to toweling off the dishes in silence, eyes respectfully downcast.

Both girls looked up when Sophia came in. She had taken off her heels and jewelry, which she always looked uncomfortable wearing, and let her hair down. Now she walked over to Amy and gently pulled on the towel as if to remove it from her daughter's hands. Amy kept a firm grip on it, however, and after a second or two, Sophia let go, looking embarrassed.

"Why are you doing that, darling?" she murmured. "Your sister seems to have things under control. Come into the parlor and have some coffee with me. I want to talk to you."

"Why?" Amy hadn't really wanted to dry the dishes in the first place, but now that her mother had asked her to stop, there was no way she was leaving until every fish fork was bone dry. "I'm enjoying myself."

Sophia sighed. "Amy—" she began, but Amy cut her off with an annoyed look.

"Mother, why aren't you in the library with Granny and Aunt Victoria? We were about to bring in the tea and coffee."

Sophia shifted and looked down. "It seems that they have a few matters to discuss in private. I didn't want to intrude. And John is relaxing alone in his study. It's been such a stressful day."

"Stressful?" This time Tanya cut in. "You mean our uncle— your brother-in-law—dropping dead right in front of us?" Tanya turned around to face Sophia, who looked as shocked as Amy had at Tanya's uncharacteristic vehemence. Tanya's eyes were bright and her cheeks were tinged pink. Her voice rose higher and higher as she continued. "Yes, it's *very* stressful when a member of your family is poisoned at Thanksgiving dinner. Perhaps we should all relax for a little while—sip some tea, get a massage, have a stiff drink, take some pills…anything so we won't have to think! That usually does the trick, right?"

Tanya sounded close to hysteria. Sophia and Amy looked at each other. A small smile played around Amy's mouth, but Sophia looked deeply uncomfortable.

"Relax, Tanya." Amy took the sponge from her half sister and started lathering the dishes. "That's not what my mother meant." Of course, it was exactly what Sophia had meant, but Amy didn't feel like prolonging Tanya's hysteria, no matter how amusing it was. To steer everyone toward where all the action was happening, Amy smiled sweetly and kissed her mother on the cheek. "It *has* been a rough day, Mother. Why don't you go ahead to the library? I'll be in soon with the tray."

A look of happy relief washed over Sophia's face. Nodding, she walked away. Throwing a half-annoyed, half-impressed look in Tanya's direction, Amy threw down the sponge and began preparing the silver coffee tray. Tanya took a deep breath and began scrubbing again.

❊ ❊ ❊

Sophia hadn't grown up in a mansion like Harwood House. Her house had been a ramshackle clapboard cottage, white, with bright red flower boxes in the windows. It had overflowed with children, pets, and two overworked parents. Sophia had never been ambitious, and had never yearned for money or power or anything of the sort. All she'd ever wanted, throughout her remarkably unremarkable childhood, was a family. Sophia was the middle child, with three older and three younger siblings. Consequently, she had missed out on both the focused attention afforded the elder children and the spoiled fun enjoyed by the younger children, and often wondered if her family had noticed her at all. She dreamed of having a family of her own—children to care for, a husband to love. She hadn't expected to marry rich; a tradesman or blue-collar worker would have suited her fine. All she wanted was to love and be loved.

Growing up in a town as small as theirs, Sophia had, of course, heard of the Harwood family, but she never involved herself with gossip and the stories that swirled around the famous name. Victoria and John James were like television characters to her; why should she care whom they married? It was all so irrelevant to her simple life, so far removed that it hardly registered. Somewhere, some rich boy had peacocks strutting around at a party. His new wife wore a fancy white dress. Big deal. When she saw the wedding announcement of John James and Catherine in the local newspaper, she had daydreamed a little wistfully of the perfect life such people would lead, and then thought no more about it.

Then several years later, after Catherine's death, she had met John James, quite by accident, walking through the local park. She was more than a little star struck.

Dating John James had been like something out of a slightly twisted fairy tale. Everything appeared as it should have, on the surface—expensive dinners at the best restaurants in town, extravagant bouquets of flowers that arrived at her door with handwritten notes attached, drinks by candlelight on the expansive Harwood terrace late at night, soft romantic music playing in the background. But something was missing. It took Sophia until after they were engaged to realize what that was: John James. His heart simply wasn't in it.

Sophia knew about Catherine, of course, and remembered reading about her death—the entire town had mourned her for weeks—and knew that they'd had a child, Tanya, who was now a toddler. But she had been so drawn into his world, so dazzled by his attention that she had never questioned whether John James really loved her.

On their wedding day, she knew the answer. John James would never be over Catherine, his one true love. Sophia could never fill her shoes. It was heartbreaking to realize. Sophia remembered looking at the faces of the guests as they congratulated her, and she saw the pity in their eyes, and suddenly she wanted nothing more than to run away, as far from the Harwoods as she possibly could go. Instead, she smiled and thanked everyone, and returned to the mansion as John James's new bride.

Soon Sophia had a beautiful daughter of her own, along with an unwanted stepdaughter, a formidable and controlling mother-in-law who gave her no respect, and a distant husband who was barely interested in his new daughter and even less interested in her. At first, Sophia had tried to create the family she had once dreamed of, surprising John at the office or cooking special meals for him and Amy, trying to schedule time for the three of them to be alone together. But she soon realized that John James had eyes only for Tanya, and as Sophia's efforts went unrewarded, she began to lose her spirit. She found herself treating Tanya worse and worse, and taking pills more frequently to numb the truth of her twisted family situation. These days, she barely spoke unless spoken to, and kept herself heavily medicated, for she quickly learned that feeling nothing at all was far better than anything else she could be feeling.

❈ ❈ ❈

While the girls were finishing the dishes, Granny spoke with Victoria, who was curled up on the couch in the library. She handed her daughter a strong coffee and, with a stern gaze, sat down in the silk damask wing chair.

"Now listen to me, Victoria," she said softly. "I don't want this incident coming between you and your brother. The bonds of blood in this family are thick, and there is no outside force strong enough to break them. Mourn Victor now, but in time, you will heal and you will be grateful to have your family by your side. We will all be here for you."

"How can you say that, Mother?" Victoria looked up from under her smudged eyelids. "Victor *was* my family. I had a life with him, a future…"

Granny regarded her daughter with sympathy and a barely concealed touch of skepticism. She didn't say anything. Victoria looked over at her after a moment, the beginnings of indignant anger forming in her teary eyes. "Mother, whatever you all thought of Victor—" She stopped, seemingly at a loss for words. Finally, she blurted out, "He was my husband, Mother! My husband. And now he's dead. And John—" Victoria looked at Granny with tear-stained cheeks. "I know John did this, Mother. He's always hated Victor. Even before—"

"Hush." Coldness crept into Granny's voice. "Haven't you learned yet not to talk about things you don't understand?"

Victoria blinked her huge brown eyes. She opened her mouth to reply, but before she got the chance, the library door flew open and John James crashed into the room, red-faced, clutching a glass of Scotch.

"How dare you!"

Victoria looked up, mascara-stained, at her brother's towering frame.

"John…?"

"How *dare* you accuse me of *killing* your husband? I wouldn't have wasted a *second* of my life on planning his murder, or *anything* to do with him!" John James's eyes were wild with alcohol and rage. He threw his glass down at Victoria's feet. It struck the thick Oriental carpet with a dull thud and refused to break, blunting some of its effect. Granny picked it up, wiped it with her handkerchief, and set it on the rosewood Louis XV end table without a word.

Victoria recoiled against the couch cushions and spoke in a small but even voice. "John, please. I know how much you hated Victor."

"I hated Victor? I didn't care enough about the man to hate him. He hated me! He was always jealous of me. Jealous of my money, my position at the company, my wife…"

At this, Victoria managed a mirthless laugh. "Your wife? Thanks, John. That makes me feel wonderful. And anyway," Victoria said bitterly, "he didn't have to begrudge you *that*. I know what he did with Catherine."

With another roar, John James picked up a porcelain vase next to the couch and threw it across the room. The results were more satisfying this time, as it shattered against the carved oak paneling. Granny pursed her lips but said nothing.

"Enough of your lies! Don't you even speak Catherine's name! Just because your husband was a cheating bastard doesn't mean that everyone—"

But Victoria was gathering strength. In a slightly louder voice, she continued. "Their affair? I knew all about it. If Victor was a cheating good-for-nothing, then so was she! Don't act like she was a saint, John! I *know*."

This time it was Granny who interrupted her softly. "Be quiet, Victoria. John, calm down, for heaven's sake. You're family. You should be on the same side no matter what."

But John James was unshakeable. Turning around to face his mother, running a hand through his silver-streaked hair, he shook his head almost pleadingly. "No! Catherine was family, too. And the way Victoria talks about her—" He whipped around defiantly toward his sister, then back at his mother. "It can't be true. Catherine was always faithful to me. *Always*."

He stared for a moment at his mother's steady, almost pitying gaze before turning toward the door. Just then the great clanging doorbell sounded, and everyone—even Granny—jumped. The occupants of the library waited with bated breath. They heard the housekeeper's shoes clack across the marble entryway, the door open, and low voices converse. Then the footsteps—two pairs of shoes this time—drew closer to the library, and the housekeeper knocked to announce the arrival of local police Detective William Branch. Would the family receive him in the library?

"Of course," replied John James, after a beat. "Show him in, please."

Detective Branch was a tall, lanky man with a thin mustache and shifty eyes. The family knew most of the senior officers on the force, but this man was unknown to everyone. John James frowned, wondering why the chief of police hadn't come by personally. They were friends, after all.

Victoria and Granny sat on the couch. John James remained standing, looking somewhat hostile, leaning unsteadily on the mantle. No one asked the officer to sit or offered him coffee or tea.

Detective Branch cleared his throat self-consciously. "Good evening, everyone. I appreciate you taking the time to speak with me and I'm, ah, sorry for your loss." His eyes shifted from Granny's expressionless face to John James's slight frown. "As you can probably guess, I'm here to follow up on the death of Victor Alden. I'm told that he collapsed here suddenly this afternoon during Thanksgiving dinner."

"Yes. One minute he was fine, and then…" Victoria said with a shudder.

With a scowl he said, "I understand that you've already been informed that his death was, ah, not from natural causes." He was obviously disturbed by the apparent breach of protocol.

"Yes, my lawyer told me that the coroner believes my brother-in-law took poison," said John James, lightly emphasizing the word *lawyer*. "Surely he's mistaken. It must have been a heart attack, or maybe he choked on something—"

"Sir, there's no mistake. We'll know what kind of poison soon enough, but for now it's enough to know the general cause of death," said the detective. "I'm going to need a list of everyone who helped prepare and serve the food, as well as who was in the house at the time of death, and in the hours preceding the, ah, dinner. We'll need samples of the food from the table and in the kitchen, and then—"

"Don't be insulting, young man, dinner was *hours* ago," said Granny, cutting him off with disdain. "I don't know how you were brought up, but in this house, everything's long since been cleared, washed, and put away."

Detective Branch looked at the silver-haired matron and nodded. "I see."

As John James listed the family members, the detective wrote in his small notebook. Granny glowered at him, pointedly checking the mantle clock.

"Can't this wait until morning, young man?" she said. "The timing of your intrusion is most unseemly."

The detective gazed back, his nervousness no longer evident. "With all due respect, ma'am, no. It can't wait. You see, poison almost certainly makes it murder. So I'm going to need to speak with everyone tonight. One at a time. We can talk in here or, if there's somewhere else you'd prefer—"

John James and Granny exchanged a small glance and said nothing. Victoria looked down at her hands, a curtain of long hair masking her face. Detective Branch's eyes flicked over the three silent Harwoods. He cleared his throat again.

"It's standard procedure, you understand. We need to question everyone who was connected to the, ah, deceased. It's strictly protocol in the case of any suspicious or unexplained death like…" His voice trailed off at the shrill ring of a telephone. The housekeeper wordlessly gestured to the detective and after a few moments of frowning, he hung up and paused, as if unsure what to do next. Then he abruptly stood.

"Well, that's it for tonight, apparently. I'm very sorry for inconveniencing you in your time of, ah, grief," he said reluctantly.

He smoothed his mustache. "Please accept my apologies, and those of Captain Grey." He turned toward John James, who was vaguely smirking. "The captain sends his condolences, Mrs. Alden, and sends his regards, Mr. Harwood, Mrs. Harwood. Again, my sincerest apol—"

"Tell Captain Grey thank you," John James said smugly, taking the detective's elbow and steering him toward the door. "And that I trust we won't be disturbed further during our time of mourning. Good evening."

"Good evening," mumbled Detective Branch. The house-keeper, summoned by a discreet tug on the velvet bellpull, escorted him out. When the library door swung shut behind the retreating policeman, John James, Granny, and Victoria faintly smiled for the first time all evening.

"How thoughtful. I must remember to send something to the captain," Granny said lightly. "Come now, John, Victoria, let's put all this nonsense aside and—" Her words were cut off by the sound of the doorbell ringing a second time. Just as before, they followed the sound of the housekeeper's steps to and from the front door. The voices were lower this time, and John James tapped his foot impatiently.

"Don't tell me that insolent fool is back. If he's decided to investigate contrary to Captain Grey's obvious wishes in some self-righteous crusade for justice, I'll have him thrown off the force."

There was a light knock on the door, and the housekeeper spoke in a wavering voice.

"Mr. Harwood? Sir? You have a visitor."

"Yes, yes, send him back in," John James snapped. He turned toward the door as it opened. Immediately his body went rigid, and his eyes burned as he stared at the woman who had just walked into the room.

It was Catherine.

3

Catherine had been somewhere around the age of five when she discovered that she could get a new toy by beaming, throwing her arms around her father, and saying, "I love you." Around the age of nine, she realized that if she apologized for something and acted as though she felt truly awful about it, she'd be forgiven right away for almost anything she'd done—even faster if she could get her eyes to fill with tears. By age thirteen, as Catherine began noticing the boys who were noticing her, she learned that if she flashed her smile and acted a certain way, they would pay her even more attention. Soon, she realized that they would even buy things for her, take her to fancy places, and, later on, promise her all manner of things.

It became a game to her, an addicting one. She could manipulate the board and control the players by what she chose to do or say, and by how she presented her choice. She could influence events, form or break up alliances, and even rewrite the rules. The sense of power was exhilarating. Before that, Catherine had always felt insignificant. She had always felt detached from her family—her absent society mother and her cold father—and had been more or less raised by a series of unkind old nannies who told her that her duty was to grow up to act just like her mother and offer her own children the same perfect life someday. Catherine had seen that as a challenge, and quickly learned her way around the rules. She knew how to win. At eighteen, Catherine was beautiful, poised, charming, and excelled at the game. When she met John James on that hot summer day, she saw instantly that he was her next move. Between bites of potato salad, she had secured her future.

After they married, she put her lessons into practice, instructing the staff on what to serve for dinner and greeting old stuffy people or young eager couples with poise and ease. The moves came easily to her in the game of high society. Catherine was smart and she was beautiful, but she often felt as though her life was a game with no real consequences—she made *this* move, and advanced *that* far, she made such and such a connection, and took two more steps. Before too long, the game grew boring, and she wanted more of a challenge. Would she ever fall back any spaces, or would she just keep leaping forward no matter what she did? What could she do next? What could she get away with?

※ ※ ※

John James looked as though he were staring at a ghost. Victoria, dumbfounded, looked quickly back at the doorway as if expecting to see her dead husband following closely behind. Nobody spoke; nobody moved. They were all questioning their sanity. Was what they were seeing real? Was this really Catherine standing before them? The same Catherine for whom they'd had a wake, for whom they'd mourned? The same Catherine who had been dead for over a decade?

The silence seemed to go on for hours. Then a trembling voice came from the doorway. "Mother?"

Tanya stood in the hallway, tea tray in hand, wearing an expression of complete shock. Her tiny word shattered the room's still, huge silence. Catherine gasped and turned to her daughter, hugging her tightly. Amy came up behind them, shouting for

Sophia and the rest of the family to come into the library. Granny sat unmoving on the couch, looking at Catherine with a curious expression.

Finally, John James walked slowly toward Catherine. Sounding hostile and nervous, he loudly demanded that she explain herself. Catherine hesitantly sat down on the couch, pulling Tanya along to sit next to her and pressing her daughter's hands in her own as she spoke.

She told them a long story, which culminated on the night of her "death" all those years ago. She had been young, too young, she said, when she'd married John James. She had fallen for his looks and his charm and thought she was in love, but she hadn't really known what she was getting into. On their wedding day, she said with a sigh and a faraway look, she'd been *so* happy, *so* sure that this was the life she wanted, and that she was getting everything she'd ever dreamed of. But she had no idea what it would be like to marry into the distinguished…the exemplary…the *legendary* Harwood family. Catherine spun a tale of desperation, of feeling inadequate, trapped, chained to an existence of endless dinner parties and aristocratic airs. Although she loved her family, she said emphatically, she'd realized that she could never live up to their standards; she just wasn't *worthy*.

"I realized," she said in a choked-up voice, "that I couldn't go on like that. There was so much expected of me, and I was worried that I couldn't do it all—that I would let all of you down. It had become my entire life, wanting to impress everyone with my amazing dinners and my charity events and my fashionable clothes—I just couldn't do it anymore. But I didn't know how to tell you. Everyone trusted me so much, and I couldn't let you all down."

Faking suicide had seemed like the best option at the time. Afterward, she desperately wished she hadn't done it, but she'd been young—she kept repeating that fact—so young, so clueless, so overwhelmed. She had regretted her deception almost immediately, but she had been too embarrassed, she said, to face her family after what she'd done to them. She teared up at the appropriate moments, and apologized profusely to everyone she'd hurt, especially Tanya.

Then she paused in her story and looked around the room. "Where's Victor?"

Amy started laughing. John James looked as though he'd been punched in the stomach. Victoria looked at Catherine with hatred.

"I don't know what to think of your conveniently timed reappearance, Cathy," Victoria said evenly. "But I do know there's more to all this than what you've told us in your pretty little sob story. Why did you wait so long to come back? Why come back at all? And why now?" She drummed her long red fingernails on the side of her cup. "Victor is dead. He died just a few hours ago, right here at Harwood House. He keeled over right at the dinner table. We've been told that he was *poisoned.*"

Catherine released Tanya's hands as she put her own hands over her mouth. "Oh my God." She turned to look at Tanya again and then quickly back to Victoria, who was looking almost triumphant.

"Yes, your timing is very interesting," said Victoria. "You can be honest with us or not, Cathy, but I don't believe in coincidences."

❈   ❈   ❈

When Catherine was fourteen, her mother had come into her room and sat on her linen and lace comforter, her bejeweled hands smoothing the fabric as she spoke. It was one of the few times her mother had deigned to give her advice. She had told young Catherine that in their world, a woman had to secure her own future using whatever means she had at her disposal. Catherine was lucky, she had said softly, that she had *many* assets at her disposal, not the least of which was her family. Catherine should observe her mother and the other women in her family to see how they acted when they wanted something and how—and if—they ended up getting it. She should study well how they crafted their lives and made certain choices, and how they never made mistakes, because even one mistake could bring everything crashing down.

Catherine had listened to her mother intently, her young eyes round and serious, and taken the words to heart. From then on, she had observed and imitated, learning what she needed to know and practicing everything. She practiced her kind, gracious smile in front of her mirror for hours. She watched her mother glide effortlessly among her guests, watched her commanding but soft direction of the servants, and watched her interact with every member of her family—the ones she liked and the ones she didn't. She watched her mother apply makeup and choose tasteful, elegant clothing, and she analyzed and assessed with all the drive and determination of a dedicated graduate student pursuing an advanced degree.

Catherine learned fast and well. Soon she was flying through life. Little by little, her mother's words about mistakes faded as Catherine climbed the gilded steps up the ivory tower of privilege. Little did she know how those words would one day haunt her.

4

Victor straightened his tie in the mirror, shaking his newly styled hair and giving his reflection a roguish wink. It was tiny Tanya's first birthday—one year and nine months since he had stopped by to collect a coat Victoria had left at the house and found Catherine alone in the library nursing an almost-empty bottle of wine.

It hadn't been hard—in fact he'd been shocked at how easy it had been. Victor was no stranger to the art of seduction, but he'd always thought of Catherine as off-limits, above and beyond his skill level. And yet when he'd found her alone in the library, she'd been very receptive. He chuckled now just thinking about it. John James thought he had everything. Victor had known men like that all his life, men who thought they were entitled to have it all, who took everything for granted, who thought they were worth more just because their families had buildings or streets named after them. Men who thought that people like Victor, who hadn't been born into wealth, were somehow inferior, of lower status, less worthy. The idea infuriated him.

When he'd been at school, the boys in his class had acted the same way—treating him like dirt because of who his parents were. Victor's father had been a coal miner, and his mother had worked in a diner. They were good, hardworking people, but none of that mattered to Chandler North, Holden Newcastle, or any of their blue-blooded friends. He flinched inwardly as he recalled how they pushed him around and laughed at him, making his young life miserable. Victor had made a vow then, in his youth, that someday he would have everything that those obnoxious, en-titled boys had coming to them—and not because he was born into it, but because he would take it for himself. Marrying Victoria had been the start, and bedding Catherine had been sweeter still because she belonged to John James. After she had fallen asleep, he sat awake, watching her perfect body rise and fall with slow, even breaths, and thought about those boys from school.

The affair hadn't lasted long. No more than a month, in fact, but that was enough to set him up for life. Their daughter was now a year old—his "niece" to the outside world. Victor chuckled. John James could flaunt his wealth and his beautiful *untouchable* wife and adorable daughter, but little did he know how easily that could all change. Victor was no fool. When Catherine had come to him with the news of her pregnancy and begged him to let her pretend it was her husband's child, he had been incredibly understanding. *Let them keep up their little charade.* He would have it all someday. Victor patted on some cologne, picked up the gift-wrapped stuffed bunny from "Uncle Victor," and headed downstairs to the party.

Fifteen years previous...

Victor ran his hand through his hastily trimmed hair, trying unsuccessfully to cover the newly thinning patches. His face had hardened in the past year, and a layer of stubble made him look not younger and more rugged, as he had hoped, but shifty and slightly untrustworthy. He picked up the envelope on his dresser and tapped it against the palm of his hand, enjoying the weight of what he knew were hundred dollar bills stuffed inside. "Very good, Catherine," he thought. "You can follow directions." He didn't know or care what excuse she had made to withdraw the money from the Harwood accounts. All he knew was that it was now in his possession, with more to follow. "You see John," he said softly as he examined his jawline in the mirror, "how easily what is yours can be mine?"

PRESENT DAY, TWELVE HOURS PREVIOUS

Victor inspected his gray-streaked comb-over quickly in the mirror in the upstairs guest bathroom. Satisfied, he turned to walk out of the room, patting his stomach as he went. He could already taste the delicious Thanksgiving feast in store, and he had plenty to be thankful for. He didn't know how Tanya had found out, or how long she'd known, only that she'd come to him a few weeks ago.

"Are you really my father?" she'd demanded earnestly, her round eyes searching his ruddy face. Victor hadn't known what to say. If he said no, life would go on as it had since Catherine's death. He would reap the small but tangible benefits of having married into the Harwood family—his mediocre job within the family business, Victoria's money, his increased stature in the community. If he said yes…his heart rate increased just thinking about it. He'd carefully admitted to his paternity, feeling the inner spark of ambition, cold for over a decade, flicker back to life. Here was another chance, another opportunity to claim what was rightfully his.

As he walked down the stairs toward the grand dining room, Victor ran his hand over the shining mahogany banister with a proprietary satisfaction. His plan was well under way, going faster and more smoothly than he could have dreamed. He had forgotten how easy it was to manipulate people, and how much he enjoyed doing so. He smirked to himself, thinking about Tanya's innocent little face. With her help, soon it—along with everything in the house—would belong to him.

Catherine looked around the dimly lit library at the faces of her family members and took a deep breath. "Fine," she began. "There *is* more to the story…but I really can't tell you why I came back tonight." She began fiddling with the tassels on the couch cushions. "I'm sorry. I just wanted to see my daughter. It's Thanksgiving and—" She broke off and looked up at John James pleadingly. "I'm so sorry, John. I know it's a lot to take in, and I don't expect you to forgive me or understand right now. I just couldn't be away from Tanya anymore." She looked at her daughter again with teary eyes. "I'm so sorry I wasn't there for you for all those years. I—" She stopped and stroked Tanya's hair. "I'll explain it to you someday." She turned her pleading, tear-stained face back to John James, who was looking at her with equal parts dismay and adoration.

"Catherine…" His voice came out weak, full of love. He was about to forgive her! She could hardly believe it. Catherine began to feel herself slipping back into game mode, as she considered her next move. She was so close, and now that Victor was dead, she could reclaim everything she'd had to give up.

"John, you know what we had. I regret leaving more than I can say. I've missed you—the whole family!—so much…"

"God, enough of this already!" Victoria's voice dripped with bitterness. She glared at Catherine and spoke with unsure authority. "You don't *have* family here anymore. You gave it up when you faked your death in order to leave! Now you're back? Not if I have anything to say about it."

She turned briefly toward Sophia, who was sitting in the corner looking ill, then back at John James, now standing mute and frozen in front of the fireplace.

"Come on, John. You have another wife and a new family now. Besides…" Victoria threw a daring look at Granny, her eyes flitting briefly over Tanya before continuing. "She's not even a blood relation. *Neither* of them are." She smiled evilly at Tanya. "Why should we care about people who aren't even related to us?"

"Victoria!"

Granny's warning fell on deaf ears as Victoria said in a rush, "Mother knew, John. *Every*one knew but you. Didn't you ever wonder why Tanya resembles Victor so much?"

It took several seconds for John James to take in what Victoria was saying. For most of the people in the room, this wasn't news, but to him, the words crashed down like a powerful wave, and for a moment he couldn't breathe. So it was true. Catherine *had* betrayed him with that worthless coward, that pathetic, scheming, good-for-nothing…

John James could feel his ears begin to burn.

He looked at Tanya. She did have his eyes, and he'd always thought she looked like Catherine—beautiful. But could it be? His numbness fully gave way to rage as he thought about all the pride he had taken in Tanya over the years, comparing her likeness to various ancestors and boasting that she would one day have his business savvy, despite the fact that she was a girl. To think that that lazy scumbag's blood, and not his, might flow in her veins was enough to make his own boil, and he looked at Catherine through a red haze of fury.

※ ※ ※

On the day John James married Catherine, his father had taken him aside. It would have been a portrait-worthy moment: father and son in expensive suits and ties, with matching flowers in their pockets, celebrating a joyous occasion but also securing a future for the family. For the second time in his life, John Sr. had laid a hand on his son's shoulder and told him how proud he was. Catherine was a wonderful woman, he said, who would be a loving mother to his children, and a good wife, both in the privacy of their home and to the outside world. When the spotlight shone on Harwood House, Catherine would be lit up, beautiful and welcoming, the perfect symbol. And he was certain that when he and Clarissa were gone, John Jr. and Catherine could fill their shoes perfectly as heads of the family. Of course, John Sr. hadn't said all that in so many words, but his confident, almost loving grip on his son's shoulder had said it all, as far as John James was concerned. John James had done it. The two men looked at each other, and a look passed between them that briefly softened the usual flinty coldness of their eyes.

Later that night, after Catherine had fallen asleep, John James had walked around the silent Harwood house. He ran his hands down the smooth wooden bannister and gazed up at the crystal chandeliers he had known since boyhood. He felt as if he was reaching his destiny, and Catherine was the missing piece, the key to the lock, the catalyst that made it all work together. Together they would do extraordinary things, raise beautiful children, and secure for them a strong legacy. It was all in front of him, laid out so clearly. John James wrapped his hands tightly around the door-knobs of his father's study, which had been his whole life a sacred, almost scary place, and pushed open the doors.

"Get out." Although his insides were trembling with rage, his voice was steady and hard. He looked at Catherine as if truly seeing her for the first time. He let his anger fully take over, flowing through his body and flooding every other emotion, burying the pain of her betrayal.

"Leave my house this instant, and never come back. Never speak to a member of my family again. Never contact a member of my family again. Never so much as *think* about a member of my family again, or you will regret it. Before tonight, you were dead to us. As far as we are concerned, tonight never happened, and you are dead to us still."

He took a breath. Everyone in the room was silent, their eyes fixed on John James. Catherine stood still, but she didn't back down. Instead, she looked at her former husband in a level, almost calculating way. This was what she had been expecting, after all, so she would leave without complaint. But she had one more question, and she would not leave without the answer.

For most of her life, Catherine had never known what it felt like to care about another person in any real way. Her parents, grandparents, caretakers, and various servants and maids—none of them had modeled any kind of loving relationship for her, and consequently she formed none throughout her life. She remained dissociated, detached; everything was a game, a sociological experiment. That was, until her daughter was born. Then, everything was about Tanya. Suddenly, preserving Tanya's happiness, future, and well-being was more important than preserving her own.

Catherine could remember that day like it was yesterday: sitting on the couch in front of the fire, halfway through a bottle of Chardonnay, bored to tears with her perfect life. It was all so easy, playing Society Wife. Give a dinner party here, compliment an investor there. Go to charity events, write letters, make phone calls, flash her winning smile, and always—always!—look as if she really cared about any of it. It was incredible how simple it was, really. Catherine had mastered the game, could play it in her sleep, and she was looking for a way to shake things up when Victor's leering face had peeked into the library.

"Oh, sorry, Cath—didn't mean to interrupt!" She and Victor had always been on barely cordial terms, without anything much of substance to say to each other. Catherine shared her husband's view of Victor as boring, common, and rather stupid, and Victor—who knew what he thought of her? He always seemed slightly intimidated by her grace and confidence. But tonight he sauntered over to the couch without invitation and sat down, trying his best to look concerned.

"Are you all right?" He shifted awkwardly as if to put a hand on her arm, then stopped midmotion. "I'm just here to collect Vicky's fur. Have you seen it? She must have left it in the dining room. Always so absentminded, my wife—good thing she has me to keep track of her things."

As Victor rambled on, Catherine tilted her head to the side, observing him in the firelight. Maybe it was the wine or her boredom or a combination of the two, but she decided to seduce him. It would add a risky dimension to the game, but it would also save her from her boredom and give her a power trip to boot. She recrossed her legs and leaned forward, looking Victor directly in the eyes. It hadn't been hard.

When she'd found out she was pregnant, the first thing she felt was a sense of defeat. She'd played each move so carefully, and now she'd been dealt the worst possible hand. It might be John James's baby…but probably not. Nonetheless, Catherine pulled off what she felt was a brilliant turnaround—with some masterful convincing, Victor agreed to feign ignorance while she passed the baby off as her husband's. Consequently, John James was overjoyed about the pregnancy and all was well. She was on top of the game once again.

On the day Tanya was born, everything changed. Something clicked in Catherine that she hadn't been expecting, had never even known was there. Suddenly, life wasn't about winning some silly game anymore—it was about the living, breathing thing that now depended on her for survival. The first time infant Tanya grasped Catherine's finger with her tiny hand, Tanya became her whole life. When Victor showed up one day and quietly demanded payment for his silence, Catherine didn't think about how to beat him at the game. She thought about Tanya, and she paid up. But it was a temporary solution, and she knew that she had to find a permanent one fast.

Catherine remembered the exact moment the answer had come to her. She had woken up early one morning before dawn, and gone outside to have her morning coffee on the small break-fast porch. Her hair still rumpled, Catherine had tied a white cotton robe loosely around her lavender silk nightgown and padded barefoot out onto the patio. The dew was fresh, and as Catherine stirred sugar into her coffee, the first light of the sun crept up over the trees. She recalled how beautiful it was, how calm and peaceful, and how happy she should have been. She blew across the steaming hot coffee and thought about her daughter, nearly a year old.

Tanya was the heir to the Harwood fortune. That meant security and status for her entire life. Tanya would never have to worry about work or choosing the right man to marry—she could choose whomever she wanted, and there would be a long line of suitors. She would have power, influence, comfort—everything that Catherine had played her little "game" to achieve, and everything that she now had. *Except security.* With Catherine around, Tanya's true patrilineage could far too easily be revealed. Exposed as Victor's daughter, Tanya's future would be in jeopardy. Catherine had to make sure that nothing could ever touch her daughter.

As she watched the sun climb higher into the sky and felt the warmth begin to permeate her skin, she realized that the answer was for her to disappear. If she were presumed dead, Tanya would be safe. Without Catherine around to affirm or deny the affair, Victor wouldn't dare claim that it had occurred—who would believe him? Besides, everyone would find it so appalling to accuse a dead woman of infidelity that it wouldn't matter if it was true or not, and no one would ever dare submit John James Harwood to a DNA test. Yes, she decided sadly, it had to be done. John would mourn the loss of his perfect, pure wife, and Tanya would be motherless for now, but rich and powerful someday. Catherine would win the game by securing a future for her child. She closed her eyes and tried to absorb the strength of the sun, thinking about all that she had and all that she was about to give up.

❈ ❈ ❈

Catherine looked around the room—at Amy's cold, victorious smile, at Victoria's satisfied smirk, at Granny's steady, expressionless gaze. She knew everyone was waiting for her to respond, but Catherine just stood there with bated breath.

Tanya stood silently for a moment, then drew in a shaky breath and turned toward John James. "Father, I...I mean, I'm—" She looked at her mother and then back at John James once more. "Can I even still call you father?" Her voice was trembling.

John James closed his eyes briefly and then looked at Granny; still expressionless, she gave the smallest of nods. John James exhaled hoarsely, and a look of relief came over him. Striding over to the sofa, he gave Tanya a brusque hug and peck on the cheek. "Of course. You will *always* be my daughter. Whatever this whore had done."

Catherine sighed and smiled sadly, her eyes full of victorious tears. She turned toward Tanya and hugged her daughter one last time before leaving the room and the house forever.

❈ ❈ ❈

Despite appearances, Victoria was no fool. She remembered the first time she realized that Victor was cheating on her. It was a few months after their wedding, on a trip to Barcelona. She had felt almost a sense of relief when she'd found out for sure—deep down, she'd known it was coming. Somehow she'd had the sense even when she married him that it was all too good to be true. But she'd been so in love with him that she convinced herself that she was being silly. But Victor was even worse at covering up his affairs than he was at staying faithful to her, and although they never talked about it, they both knew that Victoria knew about them.

When Victoria found out about the first one, she made a decision. A decision to stay with Victor, to lead the life she had chosen. Nobody's life was perfect, she reasoned, and she had a lot going for her. A few indiscretions by her husband were hardly the end of the world. If anything, it gave her more power over him. Nonetheless, she found herself growing bitter and jealous as the years went on and the number of affairs mounted. She looked at her brother's seemingly perfect marriage and model wife, and her hatred for them was fueled by a burning envy. But she never questioned her decision to stay with her husband. Never, that is, until Tanya came along.

Victoria had always wanted children. It was Victor who balked, who said he wasn't ready, that he couldn't handle it. Why spoil the life of luxury they led, he said, with such an arduous chore as childrearing? Someday, he kept telling her, someday…once they'd had their fill of the good life, once they'd had their fun. So Victoria waited. And when Catherine got pregnant, it seemed at first like just one more thing for Victoria to be envious about—until the baby was born.

John couldn't see it. But when Victoria looked at that baby for the first time, she knew it was Victor's. She couldn't explain how she knew, but she just knew. She confronted her husband and he confessed to the affair, to his paternity, to everything. She threatened to leave him and he begged her to stay, saying that this was the end of his infidelity. From that moment forward, he said, he would be a faithful husband. He would treat her well. He begged her on bended knee to forgive him, apologizing tearfully and profusely confessing his love. And so she agreed.

Catherine's suicide brought Victoria peace, and Victor kept his word about staying faithful to her after that. Victor's child grew up as her brother's, and Victoria never breathed a word to anyone. It seemed like the best possible outcome, and although Victoria's hatred for the child was evident, no one ever asked why. Sophia hated her for a different reason, and the two women gave no love to the baby Tanya, who grew up motherless in the cold Harwood House.

❋ ❋ ❋

Catherine left a shocked silence in her wake. Tanya felt numb. Quietly and quickly she excused herself and left the library, pressing her hot forehead onto the cool marble base of the angel statue in the grand entrance hall. She took a deep, shaky breath. How had this all spiraled so quickly out of control? Had it really been only a few weeks since she had confronted Victor about being her father? It seemed like years.

Tanya remembered the moment of discovery so clearly. What had she been looking for? A ring. A ring she had seen in an old photograph of Catherine, the one she kept in the drawer of her nightstand. She'd been studying it one night, entranced as always by her mother's classic smile and sparkling eyes. That was, until her eyes drifted toward her mother's hands, delicate and small, and she'd noticed the ring. As delicate as the hand it adorned, the ring was silver with three small diamonds set in a row. It wasn't her wedding ring, Tanya knew, and she had carefully asked Granny about it. Her grandmother had replied, with a casual wave of her hand, that Catherine had worn it all the time and that if she hadn't been wearing it when she disappeared, it would be in the trunk of Catherine's old things in the attic.

"What?" Tanya had never known such a trunk existed.

"My dear! Have you never been through your mother's things?" Was it her imagination, or was Granny purposefully not meeting her eyes? "I imagine it's fairly buried up there, but of course you're welcome to take a look. I packed it up myself. I believe it's a green trunk, and it would be on the in-law side of the west wing attic. Labeled, of course."

Tanya had wasted no time in scrambling up the narrow stairs to the cavernous attic, and—fighting the urge to go through the piles of vintage clothes strewn carelessly on old ottomans and chaise lounges—she made her way to the far room over the western ell and headed toward the farthest corner. She found the forest green trunk with the large brass buckle right where Granny said it would be. Trembling with excitement, Tanya had lifted the heavy, dusty lid of the trunk and found neatly folded clothes, shoes, a few pieces of tarnished jewelry, and even fewer photographs.

Tanya nearly missed two folded pieces of paper tucked into the bottom of the trunk, only half hidden, as if someone had meant for them to be found. She unfolded them carefully and, after a moment of studying the two sheets, felt the wind knocked out of her. One was her birth certificate. Tanya Elizabeth Harwood, it read, born to Catherine and John James, with the usual statistics of date, time, place of birth, and so on. Attached to that was a newer sheet of paper, a form on generic-looking medical stationery—a paternity test, with the name of the father listed as Victor Alden.

Tanya didn't know how long she sat there, surrounded by the artifacts of her family. Who knew how many other secrets were buried up there, in the bottoms of trunks or stashed in dark corners? Finally, she settled the items back into the trunk and closed the lid gently. Clutching the papers in her hand, she descended the narrow staircase and retreated to her room.

For a week she debated whether to tell anyone about her discovery. Who else knew? Was it possible that her mother had kept this secret from everyone? Clearly Victor knew; he had submitted to a test. And Granny must have known if she packed up Catherine's trunk after her death. Did her father know? Her father who, in fact, wasn't really her father at all…Finally Tanya couldn't bear it any longer, and she confronted Victor one day after the weekly Sunday brunch.

"Are you really my father?" She didn't know what she had been expecting. Perhaps an answer to the question that had haunted her all her life: why her mother taken her own life. Catherine had left behind a daughter, just one year old, yet all Tanya's life people had told her how wonderful Catherine had been, how loving and

kind and perfect. And how *happy* she'd been with John James...
how she was always smiling...how overjoyed she had been when
Tanya was born.

And yet, there was always something lurking under the surface. Now it made sense that Victoria hated her. She understood
now, too, why no one talked about Catherine's death. For many
years, Tanya had quietly wondered, speculated, tried to piece together flimsy bits of information, and now she had a real clue.

All she'd wanted was answers, she thought now as she stood
with her face against the cold statue. And the one person she had
wanted to ask had returned from the dead, on the very night of
Victor's death. Tanya had her answer...and yet she now had even
more questions than before.

In one night she'd lost one father, almost lost another one,
and gained and lost her mother again. She didn't know what to
think or feel, so she just stood there with her forehead pressed
against the statue, its immobile face laughing at her as it had
laughed at the Harwood family for generations.

5

"Wait." Amy's voice cut in like a knife. "Still your daughter? But father, she's not! She's the child of that…that…*whore* you called her, and that man—"

"Yes?" This time it was Victoria who cut in. "*That man* was your uncle until tonight, Amy, and will always be a member of this family. I'd shut up if I were you."

But Amy, like her father, could not control her inner fury and was less adept at hiding it. Shaking with rage, she wheeled around to Granny, who was quietly sipping tea from a china cup.

"How can you sit there and allow the Harwood name—among other things—to be passed on to someone who isn't even related by blood?"

Granny lifted her eyes from the cup and blew across the steaming hot liquid as she addressed Amy. "It's your father's decision, Amy," she said calmly. "You will obey him as you have always done. Furthermore, this is your sister we're talking about. What kind of person throws away her own sister when she has done nothing wrong?"

"This is so typical." Amy stood up, shaking out her long hair, eyes flashing as she continued. "I don't care how sweet she is, how obliging, how *good*. You've always preferred her, always! But Harwood House will be passed on to *me*, as it rightfully should be."

❈ ❈ ❈

Amy's first memory was of her father smiling…at Tanya. Throughout her entire childhood, she remembered little of her father, but the memories she did have were filled with resentment. Her father kissing Tanya on the head while Amy—smaller, cuter— was passed aside with a simple hand on the shoulder or pat on the head. Whenever Tanya did something well, John James praised her effusively, citing her mother's influence and the strong Harwood blood flowing in her veins. Precious Tanya could do no wrong. Amy, on the other hand, seemed to be a shadow in her father's eyes, always trying but never succeeding. Compared to the bright, shining Tanya, how could Amy even be seen at all?

Since Catherine's death, John James had become cold and withdrawn around almost everyone except Tanya, the sole reminder of the perfect family he'd once had. At least that was how Amy saw it. As a result, Amy began to see her own mother as a failure. She didn't know what had been so wonderful about Catherine; all she knew was that her own mother did not live up to her in any way.

One day when she was younger, Amy had somewhat naughtily posed this question to her mother. "What's wrong with you?" she'd asked innocently. "You can't even be as good as a dead woman?"

It was the one and only time her mother had hit her. Amy remembered the feeling of shock as the slap hit her face. It hadn't made her angry. In fact, she'd been impressed that her mother could show such spunk for once. But then the always-shrinking Sophia had recoiled, looking more shocked than her daughter. Brushing a tear out of her own eye, she'd turned and left the room. She was back to being the pathetic, spineless woman she had always been.

Over the years Amy had wanted so many times to provoke her mother into hitting her again, but always felt so disgusted by her mother's vulnerability that she couldn't do it. If she was really honest, she was afraid that her mother wouldn't do it—that she would cry or run away, proving that that one moment of strength had been a fluke rather than a rare glimpse into some hidden part of Sophia that showed she wasn't completely spineless. And so as time passed, Amy grew more and more cynical and bitter toward her mother's shortcomings. She blamed her mother for her father's lack of love toward her, and consequently she became enraged every time Sophia acted submissive and weak.

Although they were only four years apart, Amy and Tanya became worlds apart in disposition. Tanya grew up to be sweet and quiet, caring, the perfect daughter, but Amy also saw her as sickeningly frail and lacking the kind of strength and backbone that Sophia was also missing. Amy, on the other hand, had become cynical and devious, trusting no one and always looking out for herself. Sharp and smart, she grew up feeling no warm sentiment for the members of her family. The only person she felt even slightly close to was Granny, whose strength and shrewdness she admired. *There* was a woman she could emulate. Amy had always felt that she shared a bond with her grandmother, who possessed the very determination and vigor that her own mother and half sister lacked.

❈ ❈ ❈

"Amy," Granny said softly, "you're a fool. How many times do I have to caution people in this family not to talk about things they don't understand?" Amy furiously opened her mouth in protest, and Granny stilled her with a glower. "*Especially* people who are on such shifting grounds with respect to their, shall we say, legacy?" She fixed her gaze on her granddaughter. "Don't forget that in this, as in all matters, it would be unwise to speak hastily before examining the possible ramifications."

Amy's eyes burned brightly, but she closed her mouth with resignation. "You're quite right, Granny," she said steadily. "I should examine all the possibilities. Excuse me." Amy rose to her feet and exited the room, banging the library door behind her.

Amy burst into her room, too angry to even throw herself onto the four-poster canopy bed. She had always felt she had an ally in Granny. Granny understood her, valued her, and would be there when Amy needed someone. Now Amy paced, the bite of Granny's betrayal gnawing at her with every step. No one was going to look out for her; that was clear now. But if they thought she was going to roll over and let Tanya walk away with her family, her house, and her money, they were sadly, pitifully wrong. She was not her mother, and she would show them all what she was made of. And as for Granny—Amy stopped pacing and bent down to look into the vanity mirror, running her slender finger over her perfectly arched eyebrow—she would pay dearly for this.

Everyone in the library collectively exhaled. John James stood and shakily, gruffly kissed Tanya on the head, making brief eye contact with Granny and none with Victoria before exiting the room. It had been a long and thoroughly exhausting day. Not accustomed to suffering through such exhausting emotional dramas, John James desperately craved the sturdy familiarity of his study and another glass of Scotch. Sophia quickly stood and followed. She didn't know what to do for her husband, but she herself needed a hot bath and to be as far from Granny and Tanya as possible. Murmuring her goodnights, she left in her husband's wake.

Granny, Victoria, and Tanya looked at each other. The sudden appearance of Catherine had been so shocking and her subsequent banishment so intense that Victor's death had nearly been pushed to the back of their minds. But now it returned, slowly, on each of their faces as they contemplated this latest twist. Although they pondered the same thing, each of them was thinking something very different.

Victoria had been sure that the killer was her brother. But the shock on his face when he'd learned of Catherine's infidelity and Tanya's true parentage were so real, she began to have her doubts. He'd denied the accusation so profusely, so earnestly—and angrily—that she couldn't help but believe him. Besides, it had been years since Tanya's birth, so why act now? That was what Victoria couldn't figure out; the key events in the whole drama were all in the past. And now on the same night, Victor dies and Catherine reappears. It had to have been Catherine, she thought angrily. But why now?

Tanya's thoughts were also on her mother. She could barely remember Catherine from when she was a child—a scent, the comfort of quilted fabric against her face, the sound of her laugh. A few photographs. Almost no stories. Pieces that she'd dwelled on, obsessed over, tried to fit together in every possible way to create a person. Her mother. But as much as she tried, Tanya didn't understand her at all. A woman who had married her father. A perfect wife, mother, and hostess. A perfect wife who had slept with her brother-in-law, pretended to kill herself, and left her young daughter to grow up motherless and her husband without a partner. And now there was a new piece to the puzzle; was Catherine also a killer? But that didn't make any sense, not with what Tanya had learned a few weeks ago. Unless that was also a lie, too, in which case…what had she almost done? Tanya's mind reeled and she closed her eyes, overwhelmed.

Granny took another sip of tea. These family dramas were no good for her nerves. Her thoughts were with the banished Catherine, poor confused Tanya, and angry Amy upstairs plotting her revenge. She thought about her broken son and angry daughter, both of them searching for answers. But somehow, she realized, everything had worked out the way it was supposed to.

6

Victor confidently poured gravy on his mashed potatoes, letting his mind wander back to the moment of Tanya's revelation—the moment when the idea had come to him, unfurling beautifully in his mind like a gray silk ribbon. Once again, he had been given a rare opportunity, but this time he wouldn't let it slip away. If he played his cards right, Victor dared to hope, he could end up with so much more than a measly few thousand dollars a month. He could get the whole thing. Victor's fingers tingled with the anticipation of holding the keys to the Harwood bank accounts. He had confirmed his paternity status, hugged his daughter joyfully, and invited her to lunch the following week.

There, over char-grilled salmon, he'd spun his tale. How gradually, over the years and against their mutual wills, he and Catherine had fallen in love. He painted John James as a cold, inattentive husband who had driven his perfect wife crazy. He painted Catherine as an angel and a martyr who had loved Tanya without reservation. He rhapsodized about how much he had loved Catherine, how his moments with her were the best of his life. He loved Victoria, to be sure, he said hurriedly, but the love he and Catherine had shared was beyond anything he'd experienced with anyone else, including his wife.

"You can't plan love," he'd said earnestly. "There's no way of knowing when you'll meet your soul mate."

When Tanya was born, Victor said, he had begged Catherine to run away with him. He had thought his life would end, he told Tanya in a properly choked-up voice, when Catherine had taken her own life. He went on to say that before she'd died, she'd confessed to him that she wanted to leave John James, take Tanya, and raise her with Victor, but that she couldn't deprive Tanya of her inheritance. As John James's eldest child, the bulk of the Harwood fortune would pass to her. Catherine, unable to live a lie but determined to secure her daughter's future, had taken her own life, and Victor had lived with the guilt ever since.

The story had its desired effect. By the end of the meal, Tanya was sobbing, guilt ridden, and swearing that she didn't ever want to see a penny of that cursed money. "You should have it," she'd choked. "You lost your true love, your chance at a family, because of that money. It should be yours."

He'd protested, of course, telling her not to be silly, that the fact that he couldn't go a night without crying himself to sleep or a day without the stabbing pain of missing Catherine was something that he'd learned to live with. "Plus, I've gotten to watch you grow up," he'd said smoothly. "That's all I need."

But Tanya was unshakeable. Through her tears, she swore she would give everything she inherited to Victor when the time came. She wanted to make it legal, she said, and finally, try as he might, he could object no more.

They met several times in secret to go over logistics, and it was decided that they would tell the family lawyers right after Thanksgiving. Now Victor felt a possessive thrill as he gripped the silver knife and fork, clutched his wineglass, and wiped his lips with the white monogrammed napkin.

"Mine," he thought. "It's all mine."

7

Once, when she was a young newlywed, Clarissa Harwood had lay in the grass, leaning back on her elbows, and watched the white clouds drift over the roof of the house. The sky was a clear, pure blue, and everything, including the many chimneys of Harwood House, seemed to be in clearer focus. She played with the hem of her skirt as she contemplated this icon, whose power she felt strongly as a force greater than any other in her life. Greater even than her father, than her grandmother, than her grandmother's mother. The house held the layers of all these people, their history collected and preserved forever in the stone walls.

Clarissa's grandmother had just that day explained over tea that as a woman, Clarissa would not be allowed to direct the business functions necessary to preserve the Harwood legacy. Her only recourse, her grandmother said, as she broke a tea biscuit in half, was to protect the family through other, more subtle means. Someday her new husband, John Harwood, would be the head of the house, but she—Clarissa—would have the real power, if she knew how to use it. Clarissa had stared at the monumental structure with trepidation and resolve. She made a vow right then and there to protect and preserve the house her entire life, with whatever means possible.

❈ ❈ ❈

Granny placed her cup silently back in its saucer, and thought back to that promise she'd made when she was young. This had been her greatest challenge yet—and who would have thought it would come from an idiot like Victor? After the first time, when Catherine had come to her in tears, confessing her sins and begging Granny to help her fake her suicide, she had been as surprised at Victor's boldness as anything. She'd helped Catherine for her granddaughter's sake, and although she felt angry and betrayed by Catherine, she understood the selflessness Catherine felt where her daughter was concerned. Something deep inside her wanted to help the poor woman.

She remembered that night as if it were yesterday—the cash secretly withdrawn from the Harwood accounts, an address scribbled on a piece of paper, the twisted BMW, and, worst of all, the lies Clarissa had told to her family, causing them immeasurable pain. Over the years, consistently against her better judgment, Granny had sent photos and updates to Catherine about her daughter. And as much as it pained her to lie to her son, she knew that it was best for the family to continue to believe that Catherine was dead. She had kept a close eye on Victor in the years since then, but miraculously everything seemed to have returned to normal.

When Tanya had come to her a few weeks previous and told her of Victor's new revelation, Granny wasn't that surprised. She'd been expecting it from Victor and had been ready for it, but she hadn't been expecting what Tanya had planned to do about it. Sitting on the edge of Granny's wide, imposing four-poster bed and clutching the embroidered white comforter in her delicate hands, Tanya had sobbed and told Granny what her conscience had made her do—legally sign over her expected inheritance to Victor. She was angry, she choked out, about the fact that her true father had been kept a secret all these years, and her guilt over being the reason her mother committed suicide was driving her crazy. She was such a pathetic sight, curled up in the middle of the bed. This had to end, and there was only one way. This time, it would be the guilty party who suffered.

It hadn't been hard—Granny disposed of Victor easily and without detection, and that should have been the end of it—but something possessed her to call Catherine later that night. To tell her that it was all over—that Victor was dead, and, more importantly, that Tanya was safe. That John James would do the right thing and keep her as his heir, and Granny would make sure that Tanya's future was secure, looking after her as she always had. She'd thought that would be enough for Catherine, and when she'd heard nothing but silence on the other end of the line, she'd assumed that the woman was too choked up with gratitude and happiness to speak. But when Catherine did finally speak, it wasn't to express gratitude or happiness. It was to make another request. No, a *demand.*

"I want to see Tanya." Catherine's voice wavered a bit but the sentiment behind it was strong, and Granny paused.

"Catherine, you know you can't do that."

"Why not?" Catherine asked calmly. "Victor is gone, and no one knows anything except you and me."

"Tanya knows." Granny's voice cut Catherine off. "And Victoria knows, too. And Victoria's *very* angry about Victor, Catherine. I've been holding her off all night, but if you show up, she *will* say something to John. And I can't risk that. It would destroy him."

"Tanya knows?" Catherine asked in a small voice. "How?"

"Never mind that. The point is, she knows, and John doesn't. I'm begging you; leave it be. You have your peace of mind now. Tanya will be well looked after. And you've done enough to John. Please don't take his daughter away from him, too."

"I'm sorry, Clarissa." Catherine's voice was stronger, colder. "She's *my* daughter, too. I have to see her."

"After everything I've done for you," Granny began furiously, "you would—"

"Yes," Catherine interrupted. "I would. And I will. I do appreciate what you've done for me, Clarissa, and I thank you, truly. But I won't be kept from my daughter any longer. Furthermore, I trust that you care enough about Tanya to secure her future regardless of any action I take tonight. This is about Tanya, not about you or me or John."

"The best thing for Tanya," Granny said evenly, "would be for her to continue to believe that you are dead."

"No." Catherine's voice rang with finality. "My daughter needs to know the sacrifice I made for her. She needs to know that I cared about her."

Granny was silent.

"Good-bye, Clarissa," Catherine said softly. "I'll see you soon." She hung up.

And now, Granny thought, which of them had been right? John James had learned the truth, just as she had feared. But perhaps Tanya had also needed the full truth, needed to know that her mother had not abandoned her as a child. Tanya needed to undo her own mistake before it went any further. Yes, Granny decided. If Catherine's revelation had given Tanya even the smallest explanation or insight, it had been worth it. Tanya needed to be able to trust her family again. And to rescind anything she'd signed.

Granny had done her duty once again, preserving the Harwood legacy, but she couldn't do it forever. She would be gone someday and someone else would have to protect the family, putting the greater cause above themselves and those they loved. Granny thought about her two granddaughters, polar opposites in so many ways—the two candidates for this most important of jobs.

Amy was smart, certainly. Cunning and fierce, she would ruthlessly do whatever it took to achieve her goals. But she was also selfish, and her ruthlessness was tied to a desire for self-preservation that could prove extremely dangerous. Given the opportunity, Granny surmised, she would backstab the family for her own gain with as much ease as it took to blink her big, brown eyes. No, Amy would not do. But Tanya…She had already shown that she could put family before personal gain, misdirected as the effort had been. When Granny had first heard about Tanya's deal with Victor, she had been impressed by Tanya's selflessness and loyalty to her mother. Of course, there had been certain necessary actions that followed, but now that the crisis had been averted, Granny wondered if Tanya might be the one who had what it took to serve her family above herself.

※ ※ ※

As Victoria got up and excused herself for the night—she, too, was exhausted and couldn't wait to go home, apply her nightly facial mask, and actually ask herself whether or not she was upset about her husband's death—Granny moved to sit beside Tanya. The fire had died down to the embers, and the library looked cavernous and imposing in the dim late-night light. The shelves towered up around them and the various statues projected large, ghostly images of themselves onto the high-reaching walls. Tanya looked around the room at the giant portraits of her ancestors looking stately, proud, and somewhat grim. Tanya sank further down into the soft silk brocade sofa, turning to face her grandmother. Granny's glittering eyes reflected the fire and she began to speak in a hushed tone.

"Tanya." She placed her old, wrinkled hand on her granddaughter's young, smooth one. "A lot has happened today. I know you don't understand much or even most of it." She paused. "I'd like to explain some things to you. I think you deserve it, and I think you're finally ready to hear it.

"Tanya, your uncle Victor was a terrible man. He used your mother, and he used you. I knew when you came to me a few weeks ago that he was still a no-good liar, and exploiting your sweet nature was just another opportunity he saw, much like exploiting your mother's love for you when you were a baby." She cleared her throat and continued. "Your mother made a mistake, Tanya, and she will carry that for the rest of her life. But there was no reason for you to be punished for your mother's actions.

"I helped your mother back then even though I knew what she had done, and I did it for you. Wait—" She held up a hand, seeing that Tanya wanted to speak. "Let me finish, please. I did it for you, because even then I thought of you as my real granddaughter, as I have my whole life. I have always worked to protect this family, and when we are under attack from the outside, certain things must be done to secure ourselves. I am, of course, talking about Victor. I'm sure you understand that I did what I had to do to protect not just you but the entire Harwood legacy. Do you understand, Tanya?"

Tanya nodded, unable to speak. Satisfied, Granny continued.

"As for Victor, he was given a second chance, years ago. I told him there would be no third chance, and I meant it. Everything he told you about Catherine and him was false, Tanya. Do you understand that? They were not in love. Victor was blackmailing your mother, and she wanted more than anything to avoid hurting you. Victor knew that, and that was what he exploited. Your mother did well to trust me, as did you when you came to me a few weeks ago. I was proud that day, Tanya."

Granny cleared her throat again. She was not used to opening up this much to her family.

"You showed me that you can put others before yourself, and that you'll take drastic measures for your loved ones. Misguided as your actions were, your heart was in the right place. And now…"

Tanya looked up at her grandmother, not knowing what to feel or what was coming next. The fact that she had almost been swindled out of her inheritance by her own father seemed unreal, and yet she couldn't believe she had been so blind. She tried to focus on what Granny was saying, fighting the urge to laugh or cry or throw up, or all of the above. Granny continued.

"I won't be around forever." She lifted her hands from Tanya's and reached for her teacup again, taking a long sip. "This house is an institution, Tanya, and its survival is of the utmost importance. You were born into something greater than yourself, and the task may fall to you to protect that legacy with whatever means possible." The flames in the fire had flickered down and the embers were glowing red, deepening the shadows in the library and, it seemed, elongating the faces of her ancestors on the wall. Granny gave Tanya a piercing look.

"Family is the most important thing there is, Tanya. Don't ever forget that. Everything that I have done with my life has been for this family—not just to strengthen its place in Coventry, but also to strengthen it from within. And that is the most difficult job of all. As the heir, this task will fall to you." Here, Clarissa gave a small smile that didn't quite reach her eyes.

"My grandmother had this discussion with me, as did her grandmother before her and her grandmother before that. This is our role, and someday you will have the same conversation with one of your granddaughters. In the meantime, you must do whatever it takes to ensure that the Harwood name remains untarnished, that we thrive as an institution in this town, and that the bonds between family members remain unbreakable. Any man you choose to marry, Tanya, will likely be called upon to run the business side of things, but you should realize that even if you aren't the one in the corner office, your position is just as important, if not more so. You know about the social aspect already—the charity events, the parties, and so forth—and if you're anything like your mother, you'll do just fine. It's the other things, the private things, that require the utmost delicacy and dedication."

Granny paused to take another sip of tea. "I have faith that you'll do fine in that role, as well. More than fine, in fact." At this, Granny's speech seemed to be over, and she turned to face the fire, picking up a long iron poker and prodding a log, causing a shower of sparks to sail upward.

Tanya tried to take in what her grandmother had just told her. She had always assumed that she would inherit the Harwood titles and fortune, but she had wrestled with the social responsibilities her whole life. She knew her mother had been some kind of society goddess, but she'd always felt she was missing the gregarious conviviality gene, or whatever trait would make her joyfully host a twenty-four-person dinner party made up of high officials and snobby society types. It just didn't appeal to her. But tonight, Tanya felt like she'd gone through some kind of transformation. She'd also learned a few truths: Her mother hadn't been perfect; her biological father was the lowest creature on Earth; her father loved her; half her family wanted her disowned; and, most astonishing of all, her grandmother was a...well, she'd done something... she was very *bold*. And yet, for the first time in her life, Tanya felt like she wanted to take them all on. Maybe it was the fact that she'd come so close to losing it all—no, to giving it away—that made her appreciate it more, but Tanya listened to Granny's speech not with apprehension and fear, but confidence and determination.

"Tanya?" Granny's voice cut into Tanya's reverie. "Do you have any thoughts on all this?"

"Yes, Granny." Tanya took a deep breath. "I'm ready."

A few minutes later, Tanya got up and exited the library. If she was going to strengthen the bonds of her family, she thought, she might as well begin where the bonds were weakest. She headed up the stairs and toward her sister's room with resolve and trepidation.

❀　❀　❀

Tanya gently knocked on Amy's door. Hearing no response, she pushed open the door and saw her half sister staring at her own reflection in the white-painted vanity mirror. Amy was seated on her plush red velvet stool, not moving. Tanya sat tentatively down on the edge of her bed.

"Listen, Amy. We need to talk," Tanya began. Receiving no response, Tanya continued. "A lot has happened tonight, and I just…I hope that none of it affects our relationship. I mean," Tanya took a deep breath. "The stuff with my mother was obviously a lot to handle, and Victor's death. But listen, I just found out—" She stopped abruptly.

Amy finally turned to face her, a look of annoyed curiosity playing around her face. "You found out what?"

"Nothing." Tanya blushed and looked down. "All I'm trying to say, Amy, is that I hope that we're okay—I mean, as okay as we ever are. I know we haven't always had the best relationship, but I'd like for us to be closer in the future."

"Why?" Amy interrupted. "Why now?"

"Well…" Tanya played with the edge of Amy's bedspread. She'd never been good at confrontation with Amy, despite her age advantage. Now she stammered, at a loss, until Amy impatiently blew out a breath and turned her chair around to face Tanya directly.

"Oh my God, Tanya, just spit it out!" Amy could feel her anger getting the better of her. Whatever Tanya had come up here to say, Amy was in no mood for it, and she didn't think she could take anymore of Tanya mumbling her stupid peace offering between stutters and blushes. "I really don't know what you have to say that could possibly make any difference right now. You're the heir. You're not related to me at all, to any of us, yet somehow you're the heir to our family fortune. That is so unfair I don't even know what to think. I'm officially second, in the eyes of my family, to someone who's just a lucky, random person with two shitty lying parents with no blood relation."

"But—"

Tanya's eyes filled with tears, which only served to fuel Amy's rage. "Look at you crying. It's pathetic! You should be yelling furiously at me! Honestly, you're so much like my mother…" Amy was trembling with anger. "It's not fair. My mother is so weak, letting everyone control her all the time. At least your mother had the guts to fake her own death to get what she wanted. You would never do something like that." She glared at Tanya. "You should have had my mother, and I should have had yours!"

Tanya took a deep breath and swallowed her tears. She got up, smoothed the wrinkles in the comforter, and walked toward the door. Before she got there, she turned back to look at her younger sister, a quaking ball of fury with nothing to do about it.

"No, you're exactly like your mother," Tanya said. "You have opposite personalities, but in the end, neither of you understands how to get where you want to be. Sophia lets everyone walk all over her, while you push everyone away with meanness and spite. In the end, the result is the same. And what's more, you don't really care about the family. You want their approval and their love, but do you honestly *care* about them? About anything other than yourself?" Tanya's voice got stronger as she built up courage. "You wonder why no one wants the future of the family in your hands. What have those hands ever done besides serve you?"

She turned and left the room, leaving a silent, shocked Amy behind her.

❈ ❈ ❈

Tanya walked down the grand staircase, taking shaky deep breaths. So much for strengthening bonds. But if she couldn't do that, she reasoned, she would damn well show her newfound strength. Gone were the days when Tanya would be pushed around by Amy, feeling guilty about her preferential treatment from their father and her status as the heir. She would act like a true Harwood woman—smart, assertive, confident. She would live up to her family name, and work to protect it as it had protected her.

As she walked through the marble entryway, for the first time she really looked around the house—at the vaulted ceilings, at the grand mahogany staircase, at the paintings of her ancestors on the walls. She had a lot to think about, certainly, and a lot of questions that needed answers. But she also had the overwhelming feeling of being at home. She had never turned to the house for comfort before; in fact, she had been trying to escape it all her life. But now, when she had almost lost it *twice*, things felt different.

She passed by her father's study. The door was slightly ajar, the room dimly lit with a soft green light. Tanya pushed the door open slowly and held her breath as her eyes swept over the plush leather couches, the imposing desk, and the wall-to-wall bookshelves. It was a powerful room, and Tanya felt the presence of the Harwood legacy as she had never felt it before. It gave her strength, and she stood there for a long time, looking around the room and taking in the energy of her ancestors.

8

John James gripped the carving knife firmly in his hand and took a deep breath. It should have been a good year. Business was booming, his children were behaving themselves, Sophia was still beautiful, and, to the outside world, John James remained the powerful, cool, confident man he had always been. But in reality, he was completely changed. No longer the assertive head of the household, John James barely spoke to anyone in the family save for Granny. The events of exactly one year ago had broken something in him, and now he spent much of his time locked in his office drinking Scotch, a glazed look in his eyes. He ran a finger along the cool steel of the knife and fought the urge to drag it across his own flesh instead of that of the tender, juicy turkey.

"Shall we say what we're thankful for?" Sophia's voice cut melodically into John James's dark thoughts. He turned abruptly toward his wife and nodded.

Placing her hands on the table in front of her, Sophia looked expectantly around the table. Sophia had changed as well, although her transformation was much more visible. Today she wore her hair piled on top of her head, bright red lipstick, and a jeweled necklace, and sat with her head held high. She seemed to have absorbed the confidence that John James had lost, and the family wasn't surprised at all when she gently tugged the knife out of her husband's hands and placed it back on the platter.

"I'll go first." Her eyes lingered briefly on the deadened look in her husband's eyes before she smiled and continued. "I want to thank all of you, specifically, for the support you've given John and me in the past year. We can't begin to tell you how appreciative we are. Every family goes through difficult phases, and we are very blessed to be the heads of a family as understanding and caring as this one." She paused and looked around the table deliberately. "Thank you. All of you."

Tanya fought the urge to roll her eyes as she listened to Sophia's proclamation. Every chance she got these days, Sophia tried to assert herself as the matriarch—she and John thought this, she and John had such and such a responsibility, she and John announced whatever—proclaiming the couple's role as the heads of Harwood House. It was more than slightly pathetic, given that Sophia had no real power at all. It was just a desperate attempt to create a legacy for her daughter, Amy. Tanya folded her hands in her lap and stole a sideways look at Granny, her lips twisting into a smile at the almost comical look of disgust on the old woman's face.

Next to Tanya, Victoria sat almost as silently as her brother, her wide red lips and lidded eyes as carefully made up as ever but her face unusually subdued. She almost hadn't accepted the invitation to Thanksgiving dinner, and if it hadn't for one person's impassioned entreaty, she probably wouldn't have. The memory of the previous year was still fresh in her mind and she was more than a little nervous, especially given the current tensions. But her curiosity had been strongly piqued, and so there she sat, curtains of hair falling over her shoulders, fingers twisting around the stem of her wineglass, waiting for something to happen.

Amy, home from her first year of boarding school, sat quietly and respectfully. Since her drastic, ill-advised, and completely failed revenge attempt had caused her to be promptly shipped off—against Sophia's meek objections—to a school several states away, Amy had returned to the house only once. She barely spoke during the meal, but everyone noticed her cardinal red hair, dragon tattoo, and tongue piercing. Clearly, Amy had found new ways to rebel.

Tanya sat to Granny's right wearing her grandmother's pearl necklace. She wore her hair in an elaborate updo and kept her makeup understated, selecting a pale pink lipstick to go with her simple white embroidered dress. She'd been accompanying Granny to various social events over the past year, meeting people who had known her mother and who had nothing but good things to say about Catherine. Any inner conflict that Tanya had about being the official Harwood heir, with all its responsibilities, was lessened each time she heard about the things that her mother had done, whether it was a wildly elaborate and fantastic party she'd thrown or record-setting fundraiser she'd conducted for the community center's after-school program. This was her destiny: to follow in her mother's footsteps. Except that Tanya wouldn't make the same mistakes her mother had.

Tanya tried to channel Catherine's energy whenever she threw herself into this work. From time to time, however, she would think about her other role—the one she'd accepted during that conversation in the library with Granny a year earlier—and wonder whether, when the time came, she really would have what it took to put family above all.

The meal proceeded uneventfully. John James gripped his knife in his hand and drank deeply from his glass. Sophia attempted awkwardly and brightly to engage first Amy, then Victoria, in conversation, failing on both accounts. Granny and Tanya chatted about the upcoming firemen's benefit gala. Everyone occasionally murmured their appreciation for the delicious Thanksgiving feast, avoiding any talk of the deadly poison that had seasoned one man's dish twelve months earlier. The police investigation having been effectively quashed by several curiously well-timed donations, only two people at the table knew by whose hand Victor had breathed his last.

After the meal was over, the family retreated to the library for their customary coffee and tea by the fire. The fire leapt high, and there was a comforting familiarity in the air. Despite their differences, the family instinctively reconvened there each year.

❈ ❈ ❈

Clarissa Harwood looked around the room at her family, her legacy. The past year had been hard on everyone, but dear Granny had been up to the task of guarding and guiding the Harwoods. Her decades of dedicated circumspection and course correction had served them all well, and would continue to do so until Tanya was fully ready to step in.

Nonetheless, there was now a glimmer of something changed in each of them. Granny studied her daughter. Victoria, who once would have taken the opportunity to boast about some silly thing, demanding everyone's attention, now sat almost diffidently, biting her lip and allowing a curtain of curled hair—back to its natural color—to fall over her face. Although they'd seen less of her over the past year, when she had joined them for family gatherings or at public events, she'd seemed less bitter, less filled with anger every time they saw her. Word was that she'd even taken up gardening; she'd found great joy and therapy by replacing the invasive weed that was Victor with an organic herb garden.

John James faced the fireplace, his expression intense and unreadable. It broke Granny's heart to see her son like that, but she knew that soon enough John James would be his old self. No Harwood was ever allowed to hide behind a bottle for long, and she suspected that the invitation he was about to receive to run for the open seat in the state house would put a new spring in his step.

Sophia was curled up on the couch, and Granny saw a determined glint in her eyes that hadn't always been there. The woman remained insufferably dull, but at least she had stopped medicating herself into oblivion. It would be necessary, of course, to remind Sophia that any real interference would lead to the media's miraculous discovery that Catherine was still alive, effectively nullifying her own marriage into the Harwood family.

John's daughter Amy had matured, her outlandish appearance to the contrary. At dinner she hadn't lashed out even once at anyone, and now she sat in the huge wing chair, her coffee no doubt gone cold, completely absorbed by her thick book on political theory. It would be worth watching to see whether this was a passing interest or the beginning of a new path to a different kind of power. Either way, Granny actually approved.

Tanya, Granny noticed, also stared into the fire, looking uncharacteristically calculating. She'd matured, too, although Granny would have to find some way to remind her chosen successor not to be so focused on the short term. Like Catherine, Tanya still tended to think like a checkers player, but this game of life required the finesse and strategy of a chess master.

Clarissa was satisfied. The family members were all stronger than they appeared, and each had much more bubbling below the surface than anyone would guess. Still, they needed the watchful eyes and protective power of the matriarch. Granny watched Tanya, and thought about the moment she had realized that Victor had to die. It hadn't been a choice to poison him, but an inevitable necessity, a duty like any other in her role as family protector. She wondered if Tanya would have the strength to do the same someday. Tanya had a lot to learn, but, Granny thought, as she reached for her tea, there was plenty of time.

Outside the library, the unmoving eyes of the angel kept watch.

www.ingramcontent.com/pod-product-compliance
Lightning Source LLC
Chambersburg PA
CBHW071346130626
46556CB00005B/2050